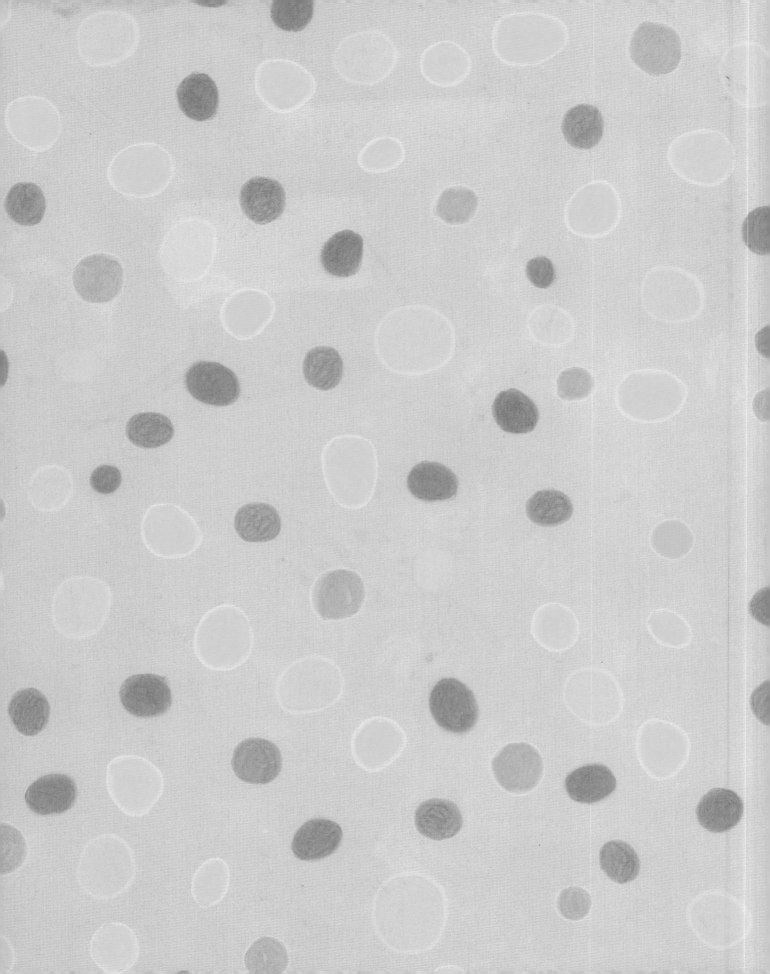

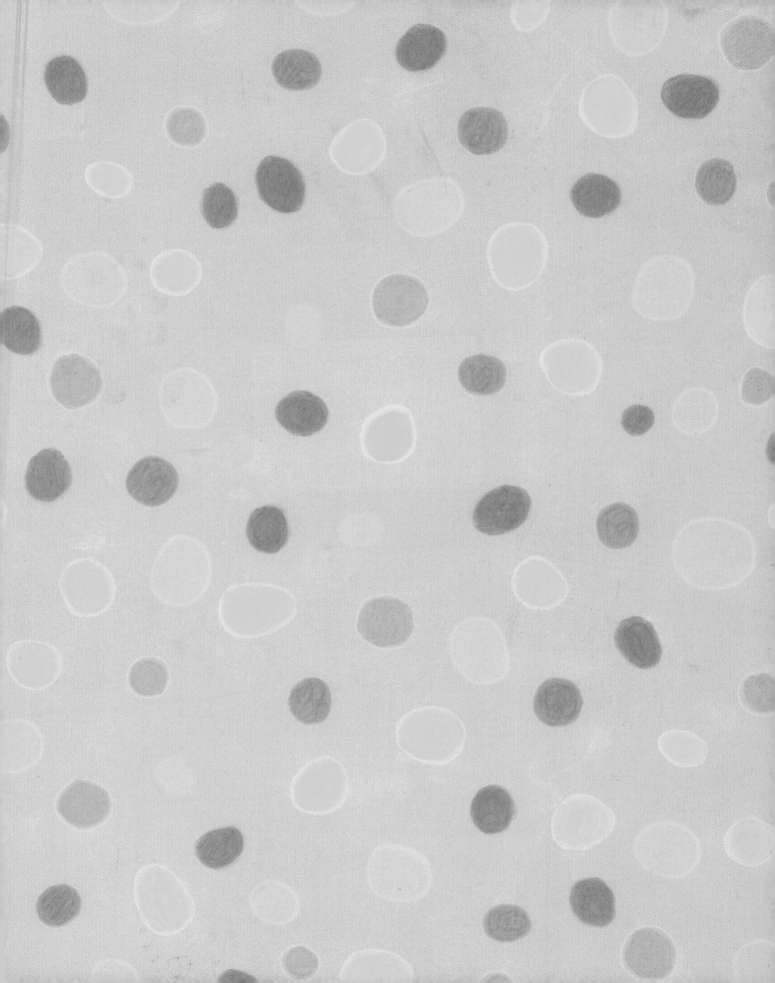

For my parents ~ G.S.

For my new nephew, Ruben ~ P.M.

First published 2006 by Macmillan Children's Books
a division of Macmillan Publishers Limited
20 New Wharf Road, London N1 9RR
Basingstoke and Oxford
Associated companies throughout the world
www.panmacmillan.com

ISBN-13: 978-1405-02210-1 (HB)
ISBN-10: 1-405-02210-8 (HB)
ISBN-13: 978-1405-02211-8 (PB)
ISBN-10: 1-405-02211-6 (PB)

Text copyright © Gillian Shields 2006
Illustrations copyright © Paula Metcalf 2006

1 3 5 7 9 8 6 4 2

A CIP catalogue record for this book is available from the British Library.

Printed in Belgium by Proost

Our
Stripy Baby

Written by Gillian Shields

Illustrated by Paula Metcalf

MACMILLAN CHILDREN'S BOOKS

There were three people in the Moon family.
Daddy Moon, Mummy Moon and Zara.
One, two, three.

But Mummy Moon said there would
soon be four people in the Moon family.
Zara couldn't wait.

"We're going to have a baby," she said to her friend, Molly. "Our baby will be just like your brother Max."

One morning the Moon family rushed to the hospital.
When they came back, there was Daddy Moon,
Mummy Moon, Zara AND Zack.

One, two, three, four.

But something was strange . . .

Zack didn't have spots,
like everyone else.
He had stripes.
The stripiest stripes
Zara had ever seen!

"Can't we send
him back and get
another one?"
Zara asked.

"No, Zara," said Mummy Moon gently,
"he's our baby. He belongs with us."
"But he hasn't got any spots!" said Zara.
"He's got a lovely smile, though," said Daddy Moon.

Zack grew round
and snuggly.

He smiled and
blew kisses.

And he held up
his arms for hugs.

"You see," said Mummy Moon,
"our baby is just like Max."

"No, he's not,"
said Zara sadly.
"He's different."

And when the Moon family went to the park – one, two, three, four – Zara didn't like it.
She thought that people might stare and laugh at Zack's stripes.

She didn't even want to play
with Molly and Max.
Because Zack didn't just look different,
thought Zara . . . he *was* different.

Molly's brother Max
could waggle his nose,

and wiggle his bobbles –
this way . . .

. . . and that way.

But Zack just smiled
and blew kisses.

Sometimes, Zara wished there were still
only three people in the Moon family.

One day Zara had an idea. She found a long scarf and wrapped Zack up in it.
"Look!" she said. "No more stripes – just lovely spots."

"But our baby's beautiful, Zara," said Mummy Moon.
"We don't want to change him."
"He's just different," said Daddy Moon, "that's all."

"I don't care!" shouted Zara.
"I don't want a stripy brother . . .

. . . and I wish he wasn't our baby!"

Zara was sad. Mummy Moon
was sad. So was Daddy Moon.
One, two, three sad people in
the Moon family.

But Zack was different.
He smiled at Zara and blew her kisses.

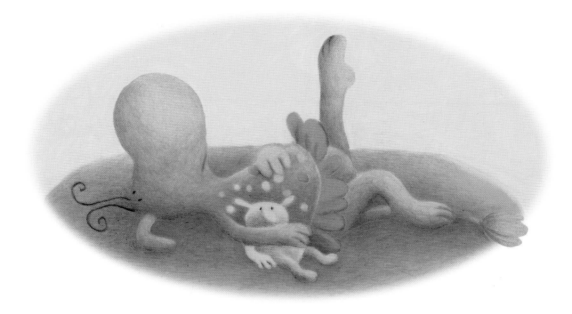

"Zack doesn't mind about stripes and spots," thought Zara. "Perhaps they don't matter."

She began to draw a picture. And as she drew, Zara began to smile.

She ran outside.
"Look! I made a
picture, to say sorry
for being cross."
"That's beautiful,"
said Mummy Moon.

"Just like our baby," smiled Zara.
Zack laughed and held up his
arms for a hug.

So Zara hugged him back.
"You're so snuggly, Zack," she said.

There were one, two, three, four
happy people in the Moon family,
playing with their friends in the park.

"This is our baby,"
said Zara.
"He's beautiful, just
like a rainbow."

And she was right.
He was.